TRIAL AND ERROR

Anthony Sauerman

Anthony Sauerman © Copyright 2024

The moral right of Anthony Sauerman to be identified as the author of this work has been asserted in accordance with the Copyright, Designs and Patents Act 1988.

No part of this publication may be reproduced, stored in a retrievable system or transmitted in any form or by any means without the prior permission in writing of the author. Nor be otherwise circulated in any form of binding or cover other than that in which it is published and without a similar condition including this condition being imposed on the subsequent purchaser.

This book is a work of fiction. The characters, dialogue and incidents are either fictitious or are used fictitiously.

All rights reserved.

ISBN: 9798337694542

Independently Published

(UK) Home Secretary, James Cleverly, joked about giving his wife a date-rape drug, just hours after announcing a crackdown on the growing epidemic of drinks spiking.

The top Tory told female guests at a No10 reception that "a little bit of Rohypnol in her drink every night" was "not really illegal if it's only a little bit". Mr Cleverly also laughed that the secret to a long marriage was ensuring your spouse was "someone who is always mildly sedated so she can never realise there are better men out there."

He said he realised he sounded like he was promoting "spiking".

His spokesman brushed aside his comments as "an ironic joke".

The Mirror, 23 December 2023

Chapter 1

'Oh, you up still?'

Rob could not hide his annoyance at finding Mary glued to the television screen at this late hour of the night, a quarter past midnight. She was always watching that bloody television, he grumbled to himself, taking over their tiny living room like a dirty smell. He had deliberately delayed his return from the pub that night in the hope that she would be tucked up in bed, providing him and his new date with some privacy. But, alas, no such luck, there she was again, almost as though she had been waiting up for him.

'Yup, still up,' she said cheerfully, her face lighting up. 'You know what it is like when you get started on a

Netflix series, hard to stop. I have been binge-watching all night.'

She reached for the remote to switch off the telly, and stood up to introduce herself.

'Hi, my name is Mary,' she said in a tone of voice that begged the question of the pretty young girl standing alongside Rob.

'Oh, hello, my name is Susan,' she replied shyly. 'Please call me Sue.'

'Sue. How very nice. Lovely to meet you, Sue.'

Rob struggled to contain his anger. The cheek of it! Butting in on his date night yet again, always hanging around with nothing else to do, no friends to visit. And on a Friday night!

He was about to say something cutting, but then came to his senses, thankfully. They were, after all, house mates; in fact, closest of friends, who had lived together for almost three years, and so she had every right to be here. This was as much her home as it was his. If he didn't like it, he could always pack up his belongings, few as they were, and find somewhere else to live, but he never did. Somehow, it was comforting living with Mary, warm and homely, as if they belonged together in a state of marital bliss; platonic, of course. Ridiculous, really, because it must have put off many suitors on both sides over the years, but that is how they liked it. Or, at least, neither of them had met anyone important enough to upset their virtual state of matrimony, such as it was.

'Drinks?' asked Mary, making her way to the kitchen.

'I think we have probably had enough for one night, thanks, Mary.' Rob did not wish to prolong the interlude any more than was necessary.

'Oh, come on, Rob,' interjected Sue, 'a little night cap, one for the road. Can't do any harm.'

Being their first date, Rob was not about to cross swords with his belle, who had clearly taken a liking to Mary, as so many did. His flatmate had a way of switching on the charm when it suited her. He just couldn't quite fathom why she felt the need to do so whenever he brought a young lady home. Strange. But a good deal better than being rude an unwelcoming towards them, he reasoned, so no point complaining.

'Oh, good,' said Mary, looking pleased. 'White wine okay?' The two nodded in unison.

Mary disappeared into the kitchen and could be heard preparing the drinks – the tinkling of glasses removed from the cupboard, the fridge door opened and closed, wine being poured, the bottle returned to its place, a call 'won't be a tic', the sound of running water, no doubt to clean up behind her, something she put down to being a little OCD - before emerging with a broad smile on her face, three wine glasses cradled carefully in her hands.

'Here we are, Sue, for you. And Rob, for you. Cheers!' She held her glass up to clink theirs.

By now, Rob had put his narky feelings to one side, and joined in the moment with his usual gusto. 'Cheers!' he called out, tapping his glass against theirs. 'Here's to the good life, and to many more.'

Mary presumed that by this he meant many more good lives, not women, though she had witnessed his fair share of them over the time that they had lived together.

They took large gulps of wine before settling into their seats, the two young women perched along the only sofa in the room, like birds on a twig, he sprawled across the floor.

'How did you two meet?'

'You will be delighted to know that we met in the flesh, the old-fashioned way, eyeball to eyeball. Not a dating App in sight,' declared Rob, sounding pleased with himself.

'Yes,' said Sue laughing at Rob's amusing description of their first encounter, 'we met in the pub earlier this evening through a mutual friend, someone I work with.'

'Well, that *is* refreshing', said Mary. 'I am amazed anyone knows how it's done these days.'

'Well, my usual charm and good looks still work magic,' joked Rob, winking at Sue.

He *was* handsome, Mary had to admit, standing six foot three in his socks, long thick brown wavy hair, perfectly chiselled body, the result of endless hours in the gym, smooth hairless torso, dark olive skin that was soft to the touch and practically repelled drops of water like mercury, the near perfect male specimen. It made living with him in such close quarters - bumping into each other in the bathroom, catching glimpses of him squeezing into his underwear or stripping out of it, having to avert her eyes as he adjusted himself on the sofa alongside her, often sniffing the pungent odour of his nether region on his fingertips - all the more challenging.

And he was charming, no question. Lovely softly spoken voice used to effect to entertain, beguile, amuse, compliment, even ingratiate, some would say.

Pretty and affable though Mary was, she could not help feeling a little inadequate in his presence. She still had to pinch herself that he had agreed to move in on seeing her SpareRoom posting all those years ago. Why me? Surely he was spoilt for choice. But, no, he had not hesitated the moment he met her and saw the apartment. 'This is just perfect', he had said, 'exactly what I am looking for. And the location, right opposite my favourite pub'.

His voice jolted her back into the moment, 'Mary, if you don't mind, we are going to slip off to bed,' as smooth and gentle as ever. 'It has been a long night, and we are both feeling a little weary.'

'Of course, of course, please go ahead. Don't worry about these things,' she said pointing to the glasses, 'I will clean everything up. Now, go.'

The clock on the kitchen wall had just struck eleven the following morning when Rob finally emerged from his bedroom to face up to the grilling that Mary would undoubtedly be putting him through, as she so often did after these overnight visitations. He felt a little hungover and headed straight for the bathroom cabinet, his sights set on a double dose of Nurofen and an effervescent tablet.

'Must have drunk more than I realised', he mused. 'Then, again, I did start straight after work, so perhaps not all that surprising.'

Sue had woken early, just after 7am, and dressed hastily, scampering around the bedroom collecting her bits and bobs – bra, underwear, jeans, top, shoes, handbag, scarf, coat – her eyes darting here and there to make sure she would not leave anything behind.

'You can't stay a little longer?' wishful thinking on the part of Rob.

'No, I must go, really. I have something important on this morning.' Her tone of voice had changed, become somewhat sharp and abrupt.

'Oh, that's a shame. I was hoping we may be able to…'

'I'm afraid *not*.' She cut him down, stressing the 'not'.

'So, coffee's out the question?' his attempt at a joke, which only seemed to irritate her.

Rob had watched her scurry about the room, a little puzzled by her sudden change in tune. It had all gone so well, he thought, one of the better ones, a real bond. Not that he was looking for anything serious or permanent, but it did make an enormous difference when there was some sensuality in the lovemaking. He had the feeling that she really liked him, but now she couldn't wait to get away. Strange.

He had started getting himself out of bed to say goodbye and see her to the front door.

'Not to worry. I'll let myself out. I know the way.' Clipped and cold.

With that, she strode out the bedroom and let herself out the flat with not so much as a peck on the cheek. Baffled, Rob rolled over and fell back into a deep slumber.

When he later emerged from the bathroom, sure enough, there she was waiting for him, Mary nestled on the sofa.

'She was *really* nice. I liked her a lot.'

Here goes, thought Rob.

'Yup, she sure was,' he concurred.

'Why did she leave so early?'

Rob could feel Mary's eyes boring into him and he wanted to run away, but he knew he would have to endure the full interrogation, see it through to the end.

'Not sure, really. She said there was something important she had to do. I suppose she hadn't banked on staying over.'

'Silly girl. Of course she was going to stay over. Why come in the first place?'

Rob bristled at the suggestion of a one-night stand. It made Sue sound cheap, and him lacking in any emotion, just out for a good time. Then, again, technically, that is exactly what it was, someone he picked up in the pub for a bit of fun, someone who was equally up for a good night with him. Nothing wrong with that, he thought.

'Well, I hope you get to see her again. I like her. You got her number, right?'

Now that Mary asked, Rob did not recall exchanging numbers, certainly not that morning. The events of the night were, quite frankly, a little fuzzy, so he could not be one hundred percent sure. He ignored the question.

'Well, I am sure you will be able to contact her through your mutual friend. She'll definitely be on Facebook.'

Rob had had enough of this. He wasn't feeling particularly well, and something bothered him about Sue's sudden departure. He *did* like her. She was very different from all the others. Yet, it was as though something had happened to change the mood, but he could not for the life of him work out what it was. Come to think of it, he could not remember too much about their bedroom encounter at all, after they had bid Mary goodnight, it was all a bit of a blur, a warm fuzzy feeling, but no specifics.

This would not have been the first time. It seemed to be happening with increasing regularity, the binge-drinking and blackouts, holes in his memory, forgetting names and faces, only for the missing pieces to fall back into place in later social media posts and pub banter. It was a little worrying. Both his parents had gone down the rocky road of the bottle, with disastrous consequences for the family, and so this really was the very last thing he wanted for himself. He figured it may well be a gene thing, passed down from generation to generation, something he would need to watch and battle his whole life.

He had shared these concerns with Mary. She had been understanding and said that she would do everything in her power to help him. But, then, she had added something about not being his babysitter and about him having to grow up and take responsibility for his own actions. He hadn't disagreed. He needed to sort it out.

'If you don't mind, I am going to slip back into my nest and sleep it off. I am feeling pretty bushed.'

Mary smiled warmly back at him, and reached for the television remote. 'Enjoy.'

Chapter 2

That was the Saturday. Just the following day, Sunday, around 8pm, there came an unexpected knock at the door that was to change Rob's life forever; shatter it, in fact. He had no inkling of its coming, and was utterly unprepared for both the velocity and the ferocity with which it destroyed the world as he knew it. Everything that he ever was, or ever had, taken away from him in an instant, never to be returned, so it turned out.

He opened the door to find two smartly dressed individuals, a man and a woman, standing on the doorstep, the man holding up what looked distinctly like a police badge.

'Robert Cooper?' he asked.

'Yes, that's me. How can I help you?'

'I am Detective Inspector Gillen, and this is Detective Sergeant Patel. Sir, you are under arrest on suspicion of...'

'What?!' Rob cut off the policeman. 'Under arrest? Whatever for?'

'Sir, please, if you will just allow me to continue.' The voice was calm, yet firm. 'You are under arrest on suspicion of rape and sexual assault...'

Again, he interrupted the police officer, 'This is impossible. There must be some mistake. You must have the wrong person, Detective Inspector, please.'

'Sir, please, calm down. You do not have to say anything. But, it may harm your defence if you do not mention when questioned something which you later rely on in court. Anything you do say may be given in evidence."

The policewoman, who was introduced as Detective Sergeant Patel, stepped forward and took Rob firmly by the arm. 'We must ask you to accompany us to the police station for further questioning. Now, sir.'

'But, I don't understand,' he stammered. 'I have no idea what you are talking about.'

'Furthermore, we have a warrant to conduct an immediate search of these premises.' He held out an official looking piece of paper, which Rob glanced at, but was in no condition to digest. 'Is there anyone else currently in the property, sir?'

Rob couldn't believe what he was hearing. He tried to work out what was going on, but he was unable to think straight. He started to feel dizzy, his mind spinning with the sound of voices droning on, the blue lights of police cars flashing in the street, the footsteps of more policemen, these ones in white overalls carrying black leather suitcases, making their way up the garden path.

'Sir, is there anyone else in the property?' the question repeated.

'Yes, yes, there is. My flatmate, Mary. She is in her bedroom.'

'Thank you, sir. Now, if you would please accompany my colleague, she will take you down to the station, where everything will be explained.'

With that, Detective Sergeant Patel led Rob to the waiting police car, leaving Detective Inspector Gillen to enter the apartment with the men and women in white.

It had been a harrowing night for Rob and Mary. He was led away, not in handcuffs fortunately, to Wandsworth Police Station for questioning, while Mary was asked to pack an overnight bag and move out of the flat while the forensics team completed their examination of the premises. Not knowing who else to contact, she had called Rob's sister, Claire, to ask whether she could stay the night. She and her husband, Richard, lived a few streets away, and so were most conveniently located; besides, she needed to speak to someone she could trust not to blurt out the events of the night to all and sundry. Being Rob's closest family, Claire and Richard had every reason to keep Rob's arrest under wraps.

'But, they can't just throw a person out of their own home. Can they?' Claire, asked, looking across at her lawyer husband.

'Well, I'm not sure,' he replied. 'Criminal law is not really my area. I presume they can. If they have a warrant, that is.'

'But, telling Mary that she must move out of her own home, that just sounds completely over the top.' Claire protested.

'Well, that's exactly what they did,' replied Mary. 'They showed me the warrant, said that the entire apartment had effectively become a crime scene, that I would only be able to move back in when they had completed their forensic investigations. They even sealed off the front door with that blue police tape, like in the movies. Oh, guys, this is just too awful. Poor Robbie.'

'Yes, poor, Robbie,' Claire shook her head. 'He must be in a terrible state. I just wish there was something we could do to help.'

'Babe, I think the best we can do right now is let the police investigation run its course, and hope that there has been some terrible mistake, that this will all blow over,' Richard, always the voice of reason.

'That sounds like wishful thinking to me,' countered Mary. 'I mean, they told him he was being arrested on suspicion of rape and sexual assault. That's pretty serious stuff.'

'It sure is,' agreed Richard, 'but how on earth could that happen? Robbie, rape someone? It's just not possible. He wouldn't hurt a fly.'

'I know, it's very strange,' agreed Mary.

Richard then turned to Mary and asked, 'Were you there when he brought the girl home on Friday night?'

'Yes, I was watching telly. They came in just after midnight.'

'And how did he seem?'

'Fine. Absolutely fine. Nothing out of the ordinary that I could see. In fact, the girl – Susan was her name – seemed really nice. They were getting on like a house on fire. Couldn't wait to get to the bedroom, actually.' She allowed herself a chuckle at the thought of it.

'But that just makes it all the stranger,' continued Richard. 'Rape, by definition, is lack of consent, but it sounds as though she was very much up for it.'

'Eager and willing, I would say,' nodded Mary.

'Did you hear anything unusual, any loud voices, any strange noises?'

'No, nothing. My room is on the opposite side of the living room, so I do not usually hear anything, but there were no loud noises, no raised voices, no sounds of any arguing, nothing like that at all.'

'How weird,' said Claire.

'You said 'usually'. What do you mean by 'usually'?' asked Richard.

'Well, just that, I do not usually hear what goes on in Rob's room. Unless, I am in the living room, of course, but not from my bedroom.'

'And what usually goes on in Rob's room, if I may be so bold as to ask?' continued Richard.

'Well, he is pretty popular with the girls. There is never a shortage of them. Picks them up... or, rather, meets them in the pub opposite, you know, the George and Dragon, and brings them home.'

'Regularly?'

Mary nodded.

'How regularly?'

'Oh, I don't know, perhaps once a week, or every two weeks, something like that.'

A different girl every week?' blurted Claire. 'But that's impossible.'

'Well, maybe not every week, but certainly every second week or so. When he is in London, that is.'

'And always a different girl?'

'Mostly, I would say,' replied Mary. 'Sometimes, it would be the same one, but not very often. He just isn't ready to settle, I suppose, still enjoying his single life. Testing the waters, so to speak. He's not alone.'

'Well, maybe not, but I just didn't think that our Robbie was like that.'

'You mean, a bit of a ladies' man?' joked Richard, winking at Mary.

'It's just that I have never seen that side of him,' continued Claire.

'Of course you haven't. You haven't lived with him in over three years. He's moved on. A changed man. And now he doesn't have to worry about his older sister sneaking around and checking up on him.' Richard was laughing loudly now.

'Oh, put a cork in it!' snapped Claire. 'I know Robbie well, and I had no idea he was so into women like that.'

'You *thought* you knew Robbie well, you mean to say,' Richard jibed. 'Who knew, your baby brother grew up and started discovering the delicacies of life, so to speak. Good for him.'

'Well, I just hope that is all he has been enjoying,' replied Claire, 'and not doing anything stupid.'

'Perhaps things just got a little steamy on Friday, too much for this Susan girl, and she panicked, ran off to the police. Who knows, she could have been a virgin, or in a relationship, and fighting a dose of post-coital guilt syndrome.'

'Really, Richard, try to be serious. This is no laughing matter.'

'I *am* being serious, babe, deadly serious. I am trying to work out what could have gone so horribly wrong on Friday night to cause this girl to report our Robbie to the police, and for them to pitch up at his place the following day with an arrest warrant. This is no joking matter, trust me. He could be in serious trouble, and I am talking prison time here. And even if this all goes away, there will always be the smell of something bad. That's very hard to shake, particularly in his line of work.'

'What do you mean?' asked Mary.

'A doctor, dealing with patients? It's super intimate. You need trust and respect. It's not like he is just sitting in an office, like a lawyer or an accountant. He is dealing with people at close quarters. The NHS and the General Medical Council will want to be one hundred percent certain that he is clear and safe, almost like he will need to prove his innocence. It's not fair, but that's the way it happens. People get presumed guilty, and then have to spend the rest of their lives proving that they are innocent.'

'That certainly is not fair,' complained Claire. 'We are all meant to be presumed innocent until proven guilty, not the other way round. There should be no negative consequences until then.'

'Look at poor old Cliff Richard,' continued Richard, 'how his life was torn apart by that police investigation splashed across the BBC, and not a scrap of evidence against him, no prosecutions, nothing. They finally cleared him, but it was years later and at the personal cost of around £3 million! He managed to get some compensation, but by then the damage had been done, I'm afraid. No, the best we can do is hope that the police treat Rob's case in confidence, and then decide not to pursue it. And we are going to have to stay shtum about it ourselves. Really, we mustn't say a word to anyone. Not unless we have to, that is.'

Claire and Mary nodded solemnly.

Chapter 3

The fallout following Rob's arrest was as Richard had feared, and worse.

Rob had been held in the police cells for the maximum period of twenty-four hours, before being released on bail. During that time, the police had conducted a thorough examination of his person, taking just about everything there was to take, mug shot, fingerprints, saliva, urine, body hair, nail clippings, samples from under his fingernails, the lot. He drew the line on semen, which they accepted – this could always be compelled at a later stage, if needed. Having thoroughly searched his clothing, possessions and body, they interviewed him under caution, for which he waived the right to a lawyer, believing he had nothing to hide. His strategy had been to co-operate with them in every which way in, fully confident that he would be able to clear his name. It was a strategy that he came to regret.

The bail conditions were harsh. He was required to pay £10,000, hand in his passport, report to the Wandsworth police station at 4pm every Friday afternoon, and keep a distance of no less than two hundred meters from the George and Dragon. The exclusion zone just happened to include 95A Western Lane, the address he shared with Mary, effectively rendering him homeless. The investigating team had cordoned off his bedroom with police tape until further notice, and so he was unable to pack a bag of personal belongings, even.

And, of course, he was not to make any contact with Susan, whether in person or by phone, social media, any way at all. As if he would, he thought, after everything she had put him through.

He took up Claire and Richard's offer to move in with them 'until the dust has settled', an expression they used to suggest that this was no more than an unfortunate misunderstanding and would soon blow over.

It all came tumbling out on the night of his release, the Monday after his arrest, sitting across the kitchen table from his sister and brother-in-law, who peppered him with a stream of questions designed to fathom what on earth was going on.

'They interviewed me for over three hours about the events of Friday night - how I met Susan, whether I had known her before, what we discussed, why we came back to the flat, whether she agreed to it, what happened when we got there, specifically what happened in the bedroom, who said what, why she left so abruptly in the morning, whether I contacted her afterwards, why not, all in minute detail, over and over again, like they were trying to trip me up, get me to contradict myself. It was awful.'

Claire and Richard gawked at him as though he were a complete stranger, anxious to work out whether he was being truthful or trying to cover up for something. Tellingly, he had not yet set out exactly what the complaint against him was, which placed them on their guard, not knowing the severity of the allegations. Richard decided to break the ice.

'If you don't mind my asking, Robbie, what exactly are they alleging you have done?'

'Oh, God, I haven't told you. I am so sorry. Everything is such a jumble right now.'

Rob paused to compose himself, took a deep breath, and, looking down at the tabletop that separated them, slowly started to spell it out: 'They have alleged that I raped that girl last Friday night in my bedroom. At least, that is what she has told them, apparently with evidence to prove it. After she left my place so suddenly on Saturday morning, she went straight to the A&E Department at the Chelsea and Westminster Hospital. She claims to have test results showing, you know….'

Richard could see that he was not comfortable saying the words out loud in front of his sister, and interrupted him mid-sentence, 'Yes, we know, Rob. No need to say.'

'What I don't understand,' continued Rob, sounding exasperated, 'rape is rape, but consensual sex is something completely different. Any girl having consensual sex without a condom will have, you know, signs of what happened, but that doesn't make it rape. I would never rape a girl. Ever. We had a good night together. Why would I even need to? It is completely crazy.'

'Crikey, mate, this is just so strange. I don't understand.' Richard held out his hand to comfort Rob, but sensed his brother-in-law retracting from his reach and recoiling into himself, as if there was something more, something he had not yet told them.

He was right.

'But it gets worse. She has claimed that I drugged her, that it was date rape.'

A deathly silence fell over the room, just the distant wailing of a siren, ringing out across the city like a wounded hyena. Claire and Richard looked at each other, nonplussed. Rob continued to stare at the tabletop, head bowed. Richard guessed that this woman would never have made an allegation of this nature if she did not have evidence to back it up, the exact evidence that she would have obtained at Chelsea and Westminster Hospital that morning. He understood the gravity of what Rob had just told them.

'Date rape!' exclaimed Claire, as if it needed clarifying. 'But, that is just crazy. I mean, why on earth would she make an allegation like that?'

'Well, according to the police, she claimed not to have had any memory of the night we spent together. She woke up in the morning realising that we had had sex, and she panicked. She claimed that I had been predatory, that I targeted her and tricked her back to my place. And she told them that I was a doctor and so would have had access to medicines. That is basically what they are alleging.'

'But, Robbie, anyone can get access to date rape drugs,' argued Richard. 'They are all over the internet.'

'Which is why they took my computer away, to see whether I have been buying this stuff online.'

'Did they say what drug it was?' asked Richard.

'No, they didn't. I am not sure they had the test results back from the hospital when they interviewed me.'

'So, they don't really know, do they? I mean, how can they make a serious allegation like that if they do not actually know for sure?' Richard sounded angry.

'The girl, Susan, is adamant,' Rob replied. 'They are going on her version of events. And she would be really credible, well spoken, well educated, upstanding individual. Why would she lie?'

'But, Robbie, you would know, wouldn't you?' The tone in Claire's voice sharpened. 'You would know if you drugged her.'

'Of course, I didn't. I would never do something like that. Why would I? I don't want to brag or anything, but I really do not have any problem getting women into bed. I never have.'

'Well, that's not so much the issue, is it?' Richard again. 'Date rape is more about control than ability. At least, that's what I've read. The person gets hooked on having control over another person, almost like having an addiction to something, drugs, alcohol, even food. But that is simply not you. I just don't see it.'

'That's really kind of you to say, Rich, but that is not the way the police are looking at it right now, I'm afraid.'

'Listen, mate,' continued Richard, 'only one person knows the true answer. We trust you, Robbie, we really do, but there is one question that I must ask you: what actually happened?'

'Well, that's the thing, I have almost no recollection of our night together. In the bedroom, I mean.'

'What? How is that even possible?'

'I don't know. I presume I just drank a bit too much and had blackouts. It has been happening quite a lot recently. I have made a point to cut back on the booze, but you know what's it like.' He looked across at his sister, who understood only too well the challenges their family had been experiencing in recent years with alcohol addiction. She gave him a knowing look, but said nothing.

'Robbie, listen,' Richard's tone changed, 'saying you cannot recall what happened is absolutely the worst position you can take. It effectively means that you cannot refute anything. You have no way of presenting your own set of facts. You become subject to whatever the complainant alleges.' He had slipped into lawyer speak.

'I know, Rich, I *have* thought of that,' said Rob, sounding crestfallen, 'but what else can I do? I really and truly have very little recollection. I can't make things up.'

'Of course you can't. I am just saying, people who say they cannot remember anything are in a really difficult position when it comes to allegations like this. You have to be truthful, otherwise they will trip you up on that.

You lose credibility. There could even be perjury, perverting the course of justice, that sort of thing. No, there must be another way of working out what happened.'

If Robbie said he couldn't remember anything, it occurred to Richard that it may well have been Robbie whose drink had been spiked, possibly in the bar, or even by the complainant herself, perhaps to cover her tracks. Stranger things had happened.

'Mate, I think you should get yourself tested first thing in the morning. I mean, no harm done. If there is something in your blood, they should find it, and, hey, presto, you have your defence. Your reasonable doubt. That is all you need. And it gets you around the memory thing. Seriously, go, but not too late, some of these drugs leave your system pretty quickly.'

Rob nodded.

The three of them continued chatting late into the night. Richard harboured a number of reservations that he held back from his distraught brother-in-law, not wanting to cause him any more distress than was necessary. The search of the flat would surely throw up signs of a drug, if there was one; the computer, too, had it been bought online. If the girl's blood really did contain some sort of tranquilising narcotic, it had to come from somewhere, and there had to be evidence of it, surely. Clutching at straws perhaps, but Robbie's only hope was that a blood test would find something in his system, anything.

Chapter 4

Things went from bad to worse for Rob in the weeks and months that followed.

The police expanded their investigation, based primarily on an interview they had conducted with the pub landlord, who told them that Rob was a regular at the George and Dragon, and that he frequently took girls home with him. That led them to believe that there may be other young women who had similar experiences to the primary complainant, Susan. Helpfully, the publican proffered a few names, but only his regulars. The police would need to dig further afield for more.

A CCTV camera aimed at the front entrance to the pub helped, but it only stored data for ninety days, so they needed to explore other avenues of information before that timeframe. Naturally, they still held onto Rob's mobile device and took great pains to sift through the various Apps and social media accounts on it. Armed with the necessary court order, access to his Tinder account proved particularly fruitful, providing a long list of young women he had hooked up with in recent years. The net was widening, more than twenty, and counting.

At this early stage of the investigation Detective Inspector Gillen and Detective Sergeant Patel were as much concerned about concealing the identity of the potential victims as they were about concealing his. He could well be innocent, certainly presumed so under the law, and so they took care to maintain the strictest confidentiality as to his association with the investigation.

Their best intentions, however, soon began to evaporate as word of the investigation started to spread and more and more young women came forward with similar stories – met up in the pub, invited across the road to his flat, leaving the following morning with little to no memory, clear signs of having had sex, and then not another word from him, not even a friendly 'nice to meet you' txt message. Why had they not reported anything? They could never be sure, they had mostly been quite drunk, some even confessed to having smoked weed or taken cocaine, or both, there was no sign of anything violent having taken place, no injuries, and nothing had ever been stolen. Some believed it to be part and parcel of the Friday night scene. A couple admitted to feeling embarrassed by the whole experience, even ashamed. They were not about to put their heads above the parapet on his account. It was understandable.

A clear pattern started to emerge, but, frustratingly for the detectives, all the evidence they had managed to gather thus far was circumstantial – none of the women had seen Rob spike their drink, none of them remembered tasting anything unusual, and, unlike Susan, none of them had thought of getting themselves tested. In fact, many even had nothing but good things to say about the man, how charming and well-mannered he was, the last person in the world they would ever suspect. One even proclaimed, 'I just don't believe it!'

It had been a process of elimination, during which the two inspectors interviewed over thirty women in all, discounting those for whom their encounter with Rob was of little consequence or concern. There were those who remembered their time with him fondly and who steadfastly refused to believe he was capable of anything nefarious; there were those who had no recollection of having met him at all and had no interest in dredging up past indiscretions; and there were those who remembered feeling a little uncomfortable at the time, but had no interest in partaking in a witch hunt (their term) of this nature, particularly if there was a danger that their exploits would be thrust into the public eye.

The inspectors did not want to prejudice the entire investigation and subsequent prosecution on a complainant who felt less than sure about her encounter with Rob, and certainly did not want to risk someone admitting under cross-examination that he had been a considerate, tender lover, and she willing. In a strange way, they felt they owed it to Rob to make sure that they presented as strong a case as possible to avoid destroying his career and, indeed, his life on frivolous accusations and finger-pointing.

They were, however, able to identify a small cohort of women, no more than eight, who had a clear recollection of hooking up with him, and claimed that they had no memory at all of what happened in the bedroom, which they conceded was worrying, even though not one of them had thought to follow up with it at the time. These eight then became the focus of the investigation, the inspectors logging dates and details of their encounters with Rob. Their stories very much matched.

Much as the police asked all the interviewees not to discuss the case with anyone, imploring them to keep Rob's identify confidential, there was ultimately little they could do to stop it from leaking. And leak it did. Rob's name swirled around the George and Dragon with gay abandon, as the regular pub-goers swapped stories with each other and speculated on who and what and how. No-one bothered to ask why. That could come later.

It was not long before news of the investigation reached the ears of a young journalist at The London Evening Standard, who managed to persuade his editor to place a small piece setting out the nature of the allegations on page three of the newspaper. The editor firmly erased Rob's name from the piece, however reference to the George and Dragon easily led curious readers to him, and word was out – *Robert Cooper, medical doctor, under investigation for date raping up to eight women.*

The two inspectors were furious, although they had to concede that the piece did persuade five more women to come forward, taking the total count to just under forty. They were able to add one of the five to the cohort, taking it to nine.

At this point, the inspectors felt comfortable that they had exhausted their enquiries, and decided to draw a line on the nine potential victims. Importantly for them, the investigation had only been able to pinpoint women who Rob had dated over the past three years. Prior to that, there were none, which provided a level of comfort that little was to be gained in digging further into Rob's past and that the investigation had indeed reached its conclusion.

Rob's meeting with the human resources manager at the University College London Hospital was anything but cordial. The man wasted no time getting to the point.

'You do know why I have called you in, Rob don't you?'

'I imagine it has something to do with the rumours circulating about me.'

'Rumours, you call them,' guffawed the man. 'I wouldn't exactly call them rumours.'

'With respect, Mr Jennings, you of all people should appreciate that people are presumed innocent until…'

'Yes, yes, until proven guilty. I know perfectly well. The problem we have here, Rob, is that we have to balance that perfectly reasonable legal presumption with our duty of care towards our staff and our patients, who have a right to be in a safe hospital environment.'

Rob knew exactly where the man was going with this, but he needed to hear him spell it out.

'What exactly are you saying, then?'

'What I am saying, Rob, is that we simply cannot take the risk of your working in this hospital until such time as you have been able to clear your name.' He paused to look across at Rob for effect, and then added as an afterthought, struggling to hide his disdain, '… which I am confident you will be able to do.'

Rob nodded to indicate that he understood the position before the man continued with his pre-prepared discourse, 'I have no doubt that the General Medical

Council will want to conduct its own investigation of the matter, and so we at the hospital will need to await the outcome of their findings, as well as those of the police investigation, before reaching our final verdict. This is normal procedure, you understand.'

There was little point in arguing with the man. Rob had seen it all before, for lesser offences, at that. The human resources director was right, they *did* have a duty of care towards staff and patients, which far outweighed the legal rights of a junior doctor subject to an investigation of such a serious nature. The key question for him now was the terms of his suspension.

'You will be suspended on full pay,' came the reply.

These words were music to Rob's ears. The legal bills would be high. They already were. He had some savings, though not a lot, and there was little chance his parents would be willing to help their hapless son, such was their revile for the predicament in which he found himself. They had all but disowned him, and asked him not to make any contact until the 'sorry saga had blown over'. Those words again, 'blown over', as though this were no more than a bad weather pattern.

'Of course, we will need to review our position periodically,' continued the man officiously. 'In the meantime, your role will remain secure, but we must ask you to please refrain from visiting the hospital or speaking to any of your work colleagues. Your access to the hospital network will be blocked and you will need to hand in your work laptop. Any breach of these conditions will be regarded as a disciplinary matter. You understand, Rob?'

'Yes, Mr Jennings, I understand fully. I am confident I will be able to clear my name. There has been some terrible misunderstanding.'

'I realise I am not your lawyer, Rob, but I must caution you to say as little as possible about the case, as anything you say can, and *will* be used against you. Besides, no-one would wish to be dragged into this unfortunate matter as a witness on account of your having told them something pertinent to the case. I say this with the greatest of sympathy and the greatest of respect, Rob, really and truly.'

Rob had been around the houses long enough to know that anyone who felt the need to add the qualifier "with the greatest respect" held little respect at all.

'Thank you, Mr Jennings. I am grateful for your support,' said Rob, polite at all times.

'I am not sure this is support, young man. I am simply doing my job. Now, run along, we need you off the premises with immediate effect. A letter confirming the terms of your suspension will be sent to you, along with your personal possessions. Follow me.'

With that, Mr Jennings stood up, shook Rob by the hand, and marched out the meeting room, looking back to make sure that the young doctor was indeed following him.

It was the moment Rob sensed for the first time that he may never set foot in the hospital again.

Chapter 5

The criminal trial was scheduled to commence in The Old Bailey a few days shy of one year from the date Rob received that ill-fated knock on the door. His solicitor, Jack Griffiths, had arranged for him to meet with the barrister who would be representing him in court, Mr James Percival of Furnivall Chambers. Rob had never before had reason to visit the Inns of Court, home to most of the London legal chambers, and so felt a little overwhelmed as they zig-zagged their way through the maze of historical alleyways and doorways en route to the consultation.

For Jack Griffiths, this was a well-trodden path. He and Percival had become a formidable pair, successfully defending clients against prosecution for a wide range of serious sexual offences, including date rape. Fortunately for Rob, the two lawyers agreed to continue representing him, notwithstanding his dire financial circumstances. Having used up all of his life savings and with his family wanting nothing more to do with him, he had to rely on the good services of The Legal Aid Agency to feed cash into the judicial slot machine, ever hungry for more. He would gratefully accept every dime available.

Following closely behind Rob was ex-brother-in-law, Richard, the only person who remained loyal to him throughout the sorry saga; seemingly, the only person who respected the legal assumption of innocence. He never once judged Rob, never once challenged him, even at the cost of his own short-lived marriage. The events of the past year had split the once-happy relationship with Claire down the middle. The moment charges were laid against Rob, she had sided with her parents, and demanded that Rob pack his bags and move out of the flat she shared with her husband. Richard objected so strongly that she did not hesitate to order him to do likewise, and the two young men found themselves a small furnished apartment in Hammersmith. Divorce papers were soon to follow.

Furnivall Chambers were exactly as Rob had envisioned them to be, a touch Dickensian, oak-panelled walls, pokey little rooms lined with ornate skirting and cornicing that betrayed the age of the building. James Percival completed the picture, a large round man of middle years, peering inquiringly at Rob over greasy specs that rested precariously on the stub of his nose, the pinstriped suit and waistcoat combination clinging closely to his rotund body, thinning black dyed hair slicked back with a heavy dose of Brylcreem, the fragrance of which clung to the walls. Rob gained the impression of a no-nonsense kind of man, a seasoned lawyer who spoke the same language as the numerous hardened criminals he had no doubt represented over his illustrious career, Cockney accent 'n all.

'Nice to meet you, young man, though I wish the circumstances were different,' a greeting he spared for those of a gentler disposition.

'Nice to meet you too, sir,' countered Rob.

'No sirs here, I'm afraid, just us, you and me, Jimmie and Rob. We are going to have to get to know one another if I am to do your case justice. Now, sit down. Coffee?'

'Yes, please.' Coffee was served.

'Right, to business,' boomed the barrister.

'Sir… I am sorry, Jimmie, if you don't mind, may I ask you a question please.'

'Of course, fire away.'

'How serious is this for me? I mean, looking at the allegations, what could happen to me?'

'Young man, let me be very clear with you from the outset, so that there is no misunderstanding. This is extremely serious for you. If the prosecution is able convince the jury, you are likely to lose your liberty.'

The room fell silent as Rob digested Jimmy's answer. His heart sank. It was not what he wanted to hear. He had hoped the barrister would put his mind at rest by assuring him that he had nothing to worry about, that he had a robust defence, and that he would in all likelihood be acquitted. But that was not to be. Quite the opposite, in fact. He faced the real prospect of time in jail.

Jimmy looked him in the eye, and continued, 'You must understand, I am duty bound to give you the worst possible scenario. Anything less would be irresponsible on my part, leaving you clutching at straws and false hope. All trials are completely unpredictable, dependent on a whole range of factors that are totally out of our control. They can go any which way, and do.'

He could see the colour leave Rob's face, the fear in his eyes, and felt the need to placate him a little.

'I shouldn't say this, but, to be totally honest, I'm surprised your case even made it out the door of the Crown Prosecution Service. And I know for a fact that it very nearly didn't. A little birdie, who shall remain nameless, told me that their case review team were far from happy that there is sufficient evidence and that a prosecution of your good self would be in the public interest. What tipped it, I'm afraid to say, was the media interest in the case, that article in The Evening Standard. They did not want to risk having every journalist in town come down on the CPS like a tonne of bricks for letting you slip the net. That is how it works, I'm afraid. And now we have to do our very best to show them that their decision was wrong.'

The speech worked. Rob felt a lot better about his prospects and settled back into his chair.

The barrister interrogated him on every aspect of the case, as though he were in the witness box, poking and probing from all angles, looping back on key points to test for clarity and consistency, all with the intention of ensuring that his client was sure of his position and reliable on the facts. An important decision would need to be made whether to put Rob on the stand. Based on his performance that day, the barrister was comfortable he would make a convincing witness, someone who the jury could believe, even warm to. He really was that charming.

They were about to wrap up, when Rob gingerly asked Jimmy if he wouldn't mind taking him through the highs and lows of his case, the strengths and weaknesses. Not something the barrister would usually do, but he was impressed by the young man's ability to process legal arguments, and, besides, he had just received news that his next appointment had been cancelled, so he had the time.

'Absolutely. But, no promises. You understand?'

Rob nodded.

'Good. To take it from the beginning, the prosecution has selected just five of the alleged victims to pursue this case against you. Now, they have the onus to prove to the jury that you spiked their drinks and had sex with them, effectively without their consent, which amounts to rape and sexual assault. And they have to prove their case beyond reasonable doubt, meaning it is our job to cast doubt on their version of events.'

He checked to see that Rob was still following him, and continued.

'Their main challenge is that most of their evidence is circumstantial, meaning they have very little direct evidence of the allegations they are making. But, they have some. Most importantly, they have the test results of Woman B, who we know as Susan, and who tested positive the following morning for GHB. She is a nurse and obviously realised that GHB leaves the system quite quickly after ingestion - no more than ten hours it is - which is why she suddenly took herself off to the hospital that morning; but none of the others thought of doing this, and so none of the others tested positive for anything. This is good. Even a positive test does not explain how the drug got there and what happened to her while it was in her system. It is no more than a factual statement that she had GHB in her system. That's why I say it's circumstantial.'

'If you do not mind my asking, Sir, I mean Jimmy, what is the significance of the fact that so much of the evidence is circumstantial?' asked Rob.

'Ah, now you are starting to get a little technical young man,' replied the barrister, smiling. 'How shall I put it? There is direct evidence of something having happened and there is evidence that allows a conclusion to be reached from a set of circumstances, which may not be as clear-cut or reliable. Even so, a jury may well be sufficiently convinced by a particular set of circumstances to rely on it and reach their decision; and often do. But, as this is a criminal trial, they need to be satisfied that the evidence is strong enough for them to reach their verdict beyond reasonable doubt. That is the key, doubt, and so the hurdle is generally higher than direct evidence. You follow me?'

'Yes, I understand, thank you. I had an idea it meant the evidence was not admissible at all, but I see now that this is not the case. Forgive my interruption.'

'No need, Rob, no need. These are important questions for you to understand. Shall I continue?'

Rob nodded.

'Now, Woman A alleges that you obtained a small amount of GHB from someone in a night club and that the two of you took it recreationally, something you have admitted to me. It suggests that you had ways and means of getting access to the drug, which is an important piece of information for the prosecution, something that is likely to impress a jury. It also suggests that this woman may well have been under the influence of it while she was with you. Again, circumstantial as far as the allegation of rape is concerned, in my opinion, but an important piece of evidence for the prosecution. Women C, D and E have not made any allegation that you provided them with GHB, or any other narcotic, for that matter. I think their cases are weak, quite frankly.'

'What clearly plays in your favour, and I will be making hay out of it, is that, despite a thorough forensic search of your flat, your computer and your person, the police have not been able to find any evidence that you bought, possessed or used GHB at home. Nothing at all. It is, quite frankly, a mystery to them, and must remain that way. Now, I have what you told me, that you have never ever in your life possessed the drug at home, only very infrequently in clubs with friends, but that is the nub of the case against you, that you somehow procured GHB with which to spike the drinks of these women to enable you to take advantage of them sexually.'

'But,' interjected Rob, 'that requires me to prove a negative. How do we prove that I didn't do something when they are all saying I did?'

'Exactly,' agreed the barrister, 'and that is exactly the challenge we have, to prove that this did not happen as they allege it did. We have to persuade that jury, and they will be naturally sympathetic to the women, I am afraid; Me-Too and all that. You just have to be yourself, and win them over, convince them that they have got the wrong guy, that you would never in your life do something like this.'

'You believe me, don't you?'

'Rob, it is not my job to believe you or not to believe you. My job is to poke holes in the testimony of these women, to bring reasonable doubt to whatever it is that they say. My personal feelings are completely irrelevant.'

The two men looked at each other knowingly. It was a naïve question, a sign of Rob's sheer exasperation.

'Allow me to finish, if I may. The real question that the jury will want to understand is why it was that all five women had no recollection of the events of their night with you, each the exact same pattern. Now, there are many reasons, individually or in combination, why a person could experience amnesia - alcohol, prescription medication, recreational drugs, exhaustion, a traumatic event, a psychotic episode, even sleep – and so my job will be to test each of these possibilities under cross examination; again, to create some doubt in the mind of the jurors. It doesn't help that you also have no recollection of the encounters, because it prevents you from putting your own version of events as to what happened in the bedroom. But it is, quite frankly, not disputed that you had sexual intercourse with all of them; what is disputed is the circumstances under which it happened, the allegations of spiking, for which there is no evidence at all, not so much as a soiled surface.'

Rob nodded that he understood the position, and thanked the barrister for taking the time to set it all out for him.

It was clear that Rob would need to place all his trust in the man who sat opposite him, James Percival KC, with no guarantees that he would succeed. His life was at stake. There could be nothing more terrifying.

Chapter 6

The trial lasted two weeks. Rob was convicted on four counts, two of rape and two of sexual assault relating to two of the women, and acquitted on all counts relating to the remaining three. The judge showed no favours, a minimum of fifteen years imprisonment. The General Medical Council wasted no time in striking him from the medical roll, and his employment at the hospital was summarily terminated, no questions asked. Life as he knew it had well and truly ended, as if it had been lined up against a wall in front of a firing squad and shot.

Richard was incredulous. He had known Rob well for a number of years, since first meeting Claire. They had gone out on the town together, sometimes with, sometimes without her, away for weekends, clubbing, pubs, restaurants, the whole gambit of social interaction, and he had never once witnessed anything unusual, not so much as a sniff of it. Girls, and guys, for that matter, really liked him, even placed him on a pedestal, like a role model, someone who had high levels of integrity and trust. Richard offered to provide a character reference for him in court, but the legal team had said this would not be necessary, that Rob's good character would come shining through. How wrong they were.

He called Rob's solicitor, Jack.

'I'm really struggling with this, mate.' The two men had become well acquainted during the course of the trial.

'Me too, big time,' admitted the lawyer. 'I am still trying to get my head around it. Of all our cases, I really did not think we would lose this one.'

'Can we meet up for a post-mortem?'

'Sure, would be good. How about a drink at the scene of the crime, so to speak?' Jack chuckled at his own joke.

'You mean at the George and Dragon?'

'Yes. Why not? Where better?'

'Where better, indeed,' agreed Richard. 'Tonight, 6pm?'

'Perfect. See you then.'

No sooner had they ordered their pints of lager and settled down into a quiet corner of the pub than Richard jumped straight into it.

'So, give me the argument for the jury.'

'Doctor, familiar with narcotics generally, admitted to buying and taking GHB recreationally, so familiar with that narcotic specifically, serial dater of women, mostly one-night stands, no sign of any commitment or feeling, slips them a Mickey Finn for kicks, perhaps even some sort of fetish, control freak, clear evidence of the two women in question having GHB in their system at the relevant time, they lose their memory, which suggests they are genuinely incapacitated, and he has his wicked way with them, no consent possible. Game set and match.'

'But, Jack, that's just bullshit. You know it.'

'*I* know it, of course. I was just answering your question, the argument for the jury.'

'It is all just too … too vague, too coincidental. Quite apart from the whole reasonable doubt thing, it just isn't plausible. There are too many unanswered questions.'

'Okay, so give me the case for Rob.'

'The prosecution has the onus to prove the crime, right?' Jack nodded. 'So, where is the evidence of Rob acquiring, possessing or using GHB for sex? There's none. In fact, no-one knows yet how that woman, Susan, got it into her system. No idea. There is just an assumption that it was Rob, but there is not one shred of evidence to support it.'

'True,' concurred Jack.

'Furthermore, why would Rob also claim to have lost his memory? It would be much easier for him to say that he remembered everything clearly, and this is what happened. But, no, he says he has no memory. Why? What caused him to lose his memory? Is it possible he also had his drink spiked, for example? I advised him to get tested on the Monday morning, but there was nothing. Of course, not – it had left his system by then.'

'True again. You should be a trial lawyer.'

'Absolutely! And every trial lawyer looks for motive. What motive does a six-foot three handsome guy like Rob, who can charm the pants off anyone, have to drug women for sex? No evidence was led that he has some sexual fantasies about bondage and control, no psychiatric reports, no-one seeing him in action in some fetish club, nothing! Yet again, a broad assumption that this is what he is into, with nothing to back it up. It's crazy, man.'

'You have hit the nail of the head, Rich. These are the exact arguments we plan on running in the appeal. But this is always the risk of a jury trial. They can get ideas in their head. There can be a persuasive juror who has had a similar experience. The way the case comes across to them can be very different from what was planned, anything. Juries usually get it right, but sometimes they can be a little wayward, which is why we appeal. The appeal's the thing.'

Just then, Richard reached out and touched Jack on the arm, looking across at the entrance to the pub. 'Hey, mate, isn't that the housemate?'

'Who?' asked Jack.

'The girl who Rob was living with at the time. Mary, I think.'

'Ah, yes, it sure looks like her. We interviewed her briefly, but she was pretty flaky. We were hoping to be able to lead her as a witness attesting to his good character, that she had never noticed anything unusual in his behaviour, and, in particular, that she had never seen any signs of GHB or any other drug in the flat. But she was incredibly vague and unhelpful, almost as though she had no interest in helping him. Very strange. So, we decided to drop it.'

'Really?' Richard sounded surprised. 'That is very odd indeed. She was infatuated with our Robbie. Claire and I got the feeling that she was actually in love with him.'

'Seriously?' Now it was Jack's turn to sound surprised.

'Oh, yes. She was always hanging around the flat, waiting for him to come home, sort of clinging onto him. It drove him nuts.'

'That's strange,' said Jack, 'he never said anything to us about her.'

'Well, he wouldn't, would he?' replied Richard. 'He was too much of a gentleman, didn't want to drag her into the whole drama. Besides, there was nothing to say, really.'

'Except that he was bringing all those girls back to the flat he shared with her. If she really *was* in love with him, that couldn't have been too much fun for her.'

'I suppose not,' agreed Richard. 'I hadn't thought of that. He said she was often waiting up for him to come home, and then got all friendly with his dates, offering drinks and everything.'

'That doesn't sound like someone who was peeved,' offered Jack.

'Perhaps she was hoping to get in on the act; you know, a cosy little *ménage à trois*.' Richard chuckled.

'Anything is possible, I suppose,' replied Jack. 'Looks like she is with some bloke. Shush, they are coming this way.'

Sure enough, Mary had spotted them and was making her way over to their table, holding tightly onto the hand of her young companion.

'What a surprise!' she exclaimed. 'Of all people, in the George and Dragon.' She turned around and thrust her unsuspecting companion forward. 'Meet Harry. Harry, this is Richard; and this is Jack. They were both involved in Rob's case, helping him with his defence.' A faint smile appeared on her face, as though she had the idea of following her introduction with a joke, no doubt poking fun at the outcome of the trial, but then she thought better of it, and continued, 'Harry is my new flat mate, moved in a few months ago.'

The two young men looked at Harry, surprised looks on their faces.

'Purely friends, of course,' she ploughed on. 'I would never want to get involved with a flatmate. Much better to keep them at arm's distance. Isn't it, Harry?' She prodded him affectionately in the chest and laughed out loud, almost hysterically.

'Much better,' he agreed, and smiled meekly at Richard and Jack. 'Very nice to meet you both.'

Harry spoke impeccable English, clearly a product of the public school system, neatly dressed, in a preppy sort of way, long curly brown hair, piercing black eyes, a handsome Mediterranean look about him, possibly of Italian descent, or Greek, but of good stock, they could see. Richard couldn't help but wonder how it was that Mary managed to ensnare such quality catches. She certainly had an eye for good looks and charm when it came to filling that spare room in her flat. He just hoped she didn't have a crush on this one, as well, or else he was in for a challenging time living at 95A Western Lane.

Richard and Jack didn't want to prolong the encounter any longer than was necessary. They made their excuses, wished Mary and Harry well, and left the pub. Once in the street, they looked at each other and broke out into raucous laughter.

'Poor guy,' said Richard, 'he has no idea what he is getting himself into.'

'Well, let's just hope she gives him a little more freedom than poor Robbie. Oh dear, I feel so terribly sorry for him. The appeal's the thing. We *have* to get him out.'

With that, the two young men said their goodbyes and went their separate ways, buoyed by the prospect of a successful challenge to the verdict.

Chapter 7

Detective Inspector Gillen and his trusty companion, Detective Sergeant Patel, had just returned from much-needed holidays, he to Spain with his wife, she to Devon with her husband and three children.

The trial, following such a complex and emotional investigation, had taken its toll on the two detectives, and so their supervisor, Chief Inspector Watkins, had wasted no time signing them off in front of their colleagues during the morning briefing immediately after Rob's sentencing.

'Congratulations to both of you on a fantastic job, a truly brilliant outcome,' he had boomed, the briefing room packed to the rafters with policemen and women eager to compliment the two inspectors on securing such an important conviction.

'I shouldn't say, but I can tell you that the CPS was none too sure about this one themselves. Didn't think there was sufficient evidence, and almost ditched the case. Well, how wrong our two stars have proven them to be, vindicating the decision to prosecute. Bravo, well done!'

The room broke into deafening cheers and applause.

'Now, unless anyone has any objection, I hereby order the two of you to take your leave of absence, the full two weeks, and disappear on the holidays of a lifetime.'

And so they did, to more cheers and back-patting.

But, as we all know only too well, two weeks comes and goes with the blink of an eye, and, before they knew it, the two police officers were back on the beat, so to speak, their phones pinging like never before. Having been off duty for so long, they had volunteered for the weekend shift to ease themselves gently back into the work routine, in full expectation of a quiet run.

It was not to be, however, their hopes dashed by an unexpected WhatsApp message, no more than two words: 'Wandsworth. URGENT.'

They wasted no time getting to the station, where they were greeted by the station commander, Superintendent Jenkins. He led them directly to one of the interview rooms, and closed the door securely behind them.

'This sounds pretty serious,' quipped Gillen.

'Possibly. In truth, I can't really say, but there is something very unusual about this one. I felt the two of you needed to be the first to know.'

'Interesting. What have you got?'

'A young lady walked into the station this morning, just after ten, claiming to have been the victim of sexual assault last night.'

Get in line, thought Gillen, very much to himself. With more than twenty-five thousand sexual offences reported each year in London alone, one more was hardly worthy of such special attention. 'And, so?' he asked, unable to hide the sarcastic tone to his voice.

'Well, she claims to have been drugged. Date raped.'

'At last count, Supt, just over two thousand of those were reported across London in the past twelve months,' he said out loud, sighing.

The station commander started to chuckle, seeming to enjoy himself. 'I know, I know, but if you would allow me to continue.'

'Please do,' nodded the inspector.

'The pattern is strangely similar to your man, Robert Cooper - picked up in the pub by some bloke on a Friday night, taken back to his place for rumpy-pumpy, if you excuse the expression, suddenly no memory of what happens, wakes up in the morning, panic sets in, hot-foots it over here and demands to be tested - blood, saliva, vaginal swabs, the lot.'

'That's what happens, isn't it. I mean, how else does one get date raped? jousted the Detective Inspector.

'Ha, now, this is where the story starts to get even more interesting,' continued Jenkins with a broad smile on his face. 'Does 95A Western Lane ring any bells, perchance?'

'95A Western Lane,' repeated Gillen.

'Yup'

'Sure, I know it well.'

'Of course you do!' exclaimed Jenkins triumphantly. 'Well, what if I were to tell you that this is the exact address where this young lady was taken last night.'

'Impossible!' declared Gillen.

'Wrong. That is precisely where she came from this morning. Had a pic of the flat on her phone to prove it. And, what's more, she had been taken there last night from the George and Dragon, no less.'

'No way.' Gillen could barely believe what he was hearing. 'Who did she say committed the offence?'

'A young man by the name of Harry. Harry Cunningham. Met him in the pub. He told her that he had been living in the flat for a few months.'

'In Rob's old room, presumably. Did she say?' asked Gillen.

'Well, thank God, she hadn't worked out the connection between the flat and the Rob saga. All she knew was that this guy, Harry, had a flatmate. Met her, in fact. A young girl going by the name of, wait for it…. Mary.'

'Shut the front door!'

'She told us that Mary was in the living room watching television when they got home, that she poured them drinks, chit-chatted and then waited for them to go into his bedroom before tidying up and heading off to bed herself.'

He paused to allow the two detectives to digest what he had just told them, and then asked poignantly, 'DI, isn't this exactly what happened with that key witness, Susan, her name, I believe?'

Gillen looked across at his partner, his face ashen. She stared back at him in horror. This was indeed the precise account that Susan had provided in her very first interview with them, more than a year earlier, and repeated under oath at the trial. How was that even possible? It couldn't be a coincidence. The facts were too similar, too detailed, an overwhelming sense of *déjà vu* about them. It was simply not conceivable that two men, unknown to one another and divided by the time and space that separated Rob from the latest protagonist in this saga, would have carried out the exact same offence in the exact same place in the exact same way. No, it definitely was not possible.

The two detectives instantly recognised that there could only be one possible explanation, one that had escaped them completely, one that meant they had barked up the wrong tree entirely, and Rob was not their man.

'Supt, can we have a moment, please.'

'Of course, of course, as much time as you like. I will be in my usual spot.'

The two detectives waited until the station commander had shut the door behind him and was well down the corridor towards his office, out of earshot, before speaking.

'Oh my God, how did we miss that?' Patel asked in a trembling voice.

'Christ, I have no idea,' replied Gillen, sounding equally unsteady.

'I mean, what a blunder.'

'Blunder?' blurted out the Detective Inspector. 'More like a total and absolute fucking failure to conduct a thorough and proper investigation as we are required to do, as we do every day of our God-forsaken lives, making false assumptions and potentially overlooking crucial evidence that was right under our noses. Not to mention sending an innocent man to jail! That's a little more than a blunder, wouldn't you say?'

The two detectives sat in silence staring into space for what felt like an age, before the Detective Sergeant started to speak, her words slow and deliberate, taking control.

'Okay, DI, let's not panic. Let's not jump to any rash conclusions. We don't know anything for certain yet, just what the Supt has told us. There are still too many variables, too much that has to be verified. We need to take a step back and start from the beginning, like we are investigating this for the first time. All bets off. No assumptions. Open minds.'

'Yes, you are right,' agreed her partner, 'no need to panic. We can sort this out. We *have* to sort this out.'

'We never interviewed her, did we?' asked Patel, jumping right in.

'Well, only briefly, just basic facts about the events of the night, but never as a suspect. It never crossed our minds that she may be...'

'Okay, fair enough,' interrupted Patel, 'but what about her room, her phone, laptop, that sort of thing? Did the forensics team investigate any of these?'

Gillen sat in silence with a glum look on his face.

'DI?'

'The answer is No. I told them not to bother. Why waste valuable time investigating the flatmate? What good could come from that? I had immediately discounted her as a suspect. In fact, I felt sorry for her, having lived in such close proximity, for so many years, to Rob, becoming his close friend, and trusting someone who…', he paused to find the words, '…drugged and raped another woman in her home. A total monster. As far as I was concerned, she was an innocent bystander to the most heinous of crimes. My heart went out to her. I didn't want to cause her any more distress than she had already been through, and so I directed the team, no need to hassle her, leave her be.'

Patel could see how upset her partner was, and felt the need to calm him. 'I understand,' she said, 'we all felt that way, no question. But do you really think that this means no-one in the forensics team ventured into her bedroom that night?'

'I don't think so, not as far as I can remember. I mean, why would they? I told them … instructed them, in fact … not to bother.'

'No photographer? There must have been one there.'

'Yes, of course, there was a photographer. There's always a photographer.'

'So, there is a chance he or she would have taken pics of her bedroom, right? That's what photographers do, right, take pics of just about everything they see, just in case. A law unto themselves. They would be failing in their job if they missed something important.'

'It's possible,' conceded Gillen.

'Well, there's only one way to find out,' declared Patel.

Detective Inspector Gillen watched his partner closely as she reached for her briefcase, took out her laptop and starting logging into her Met account.

'What, if I may ask, are you doing?'

'Patience, please, patience. This won't take long.'

She tickled the keyboard with her fingertips, manoeuvring the mouse expertly around the screen, click, click, click, until finally she sat back with a big smile on her face and announced, 'Right, we're in.'

'In what?'

'Central database of evidential digital images. The good news is that I remembered my password,' she said with a smile. 'The question is whether I can locate our original investigation folder on the system. It should still be there, and that's where all the pics will be... hopefully. Now, let me see.'

She kept clicking away, rummaging around the database until, eventually, she let out a little whoop and turned her laptop around so that the Detective Inspector could see the screen for himself. There, before his eyes, was a collection of photographs of a bedroom that he instantly recognised to be Mary's.

The two detectives huddled around the laptop and scrolled slowly through the pics, one by one, looking for anything unusual, anything that might point the finger of blame on the one person who had thus far escaped their scrutiny.

'Bingo!' cried Patel. Sure enough, there it was, staring straight out at them from the screen, in the bottom corner of a photograph taken on the night of Rob's arrest, the one piece of evidence that provided answers to all the unanswered questions about events at 95A Western Lane, the who, the how, the what and the where, a small medicinal bottle sitting on the edge of Mary's dressing table. The photograph was grainy, but there was no questioning the lettering printed on the label: Gamma-Hydroxybutyric acid. GHB.

'Henry Cunningham?' The two detectives stood on the doorway.

'Yes, that's me. How can I help you?'

'I am Detective Inspector Gillen, and this is Detective Sergeant Patel. Is there anyone else in the property?'

'Yes. My flatmate, Mary. She is upstairs.'

'We have a warrant to conduct an immediate search of these premises.'

Gillen held out an official looking piece of paper, which Harry read carefully.

'Now, if you would allow us to enter, please, sir.'

Harry stepped aside and let the two police officers enter the flat. In the street, he could see a cavalcade of police cars, their blue lights flashing brightly in the street, and a group of people milling around in white uniforms, waiting for the signal.

Upstairs, the two officers found Mary in the living room watching television.

'Mary Finnigan?'

'Yes,' came the placid response.

'I am Detective Inspector Gillen, and this is Detective Sergeant Patel. You are under arrest on suspicion of sexual assault and causing a person to engage in sexual activity.'

She sat looking at them, unflinching, and then asked pointedly, 'What took you so long?'

They ignored her question and started reading out her rights, oblivious to the fact that her admonishment inferred they may as well have been reading rights for themselves, such was their flagrant failure to uncover the truth from the start.

'You do not have to say anything, but it may harm your defence if....'

She smiled. She had heard it all before.

Patel stepped forward and took Mary roughly by the arm, clamping her wrists in handcuffs. 'Please accompany me to the police station for further questioning. Now, madam.'

Patel frog-marched Mary down the stairs towards the waiting police car, the men and women in white suits walking past them in the opposite direction towards her bedroom.

Once at the car, Mary turned to the inspector and started to speak in a soft, clear voice.

'May I ask you a big favour please?'

'I am not sure you are in a position to be asking any favours, young lady.'

'Please. It's important.'

'Okay, go on, then.'

'Please give him a message.'

'Give who a message?'

'Him. Robbie.'

'Robert Cooper?'

'Yes, Robbie.'

'Well, if I ever see him, that is.'

'Please tell him that I love him.'

About the Author

Anthony Sauerman was born in Cape Town and moved to the United Kingdom in 1995 to pursue a career as an in-house lawyer. He retired in 2020 to take up his passion for writing.

Since then, he has published three books, two relating to the work he did during his legal career and a novella, **The Box**, which is his first foray into fiction writing. All three books are available on Amazon.

Trial and Error is the sixth short story dealing with modern day life perplexities in the collection **Twists and Turns: Tales to Test and Tease**.

The first five stories in the collection - **The Pen, There But For The Grace of God, Missing, The Sins of Their Parents** and **Invisible** - are also available on Amazon. More to follow…

'Many thanks for taking the time to read Trial and Error. I hope you have enjoyed it, and should be grateful if you would please take a few moments to leave a review on Amazon."

Yours kindly, Anthony

Printed in Great Britain
by Amazon